Space Knights
and Ice
Dragons

Sheryl Webster

Illustrated by

Richard Watson

Reading Ladder

EGMONT
We bring stories to life

Book Band: Turquoise

First published in Great Britain 2017
This Reading Ladder edition published 2017
by Egmont UK Limited
The Yellow Building, 1 Nicholas Road, London W11 4AN
Text copyright © Sheryl Webster 2017
Illustrations copyright © Richard Watson 2017
The author and illustrator have asserted their moral rights
ISBN 978 1 4052 7822 5
www.egmont.co.uk
A CIP catalogue record for this title is available from the British Library.
Printed in Singapore
60878/1

Series consultant: Nikki Gamble

MIX
Paper
FSC   FSC® C018306

Contents

Knights
On Ice

Arthur the Brave and the Knights of the Round Planet were playing. Suddenly it went very cold. Was it a wind whoosh? Was it a shooting snowflurry?

'Oh no!' shouted Arthur. 'It's the ice dragons. *Again*!'

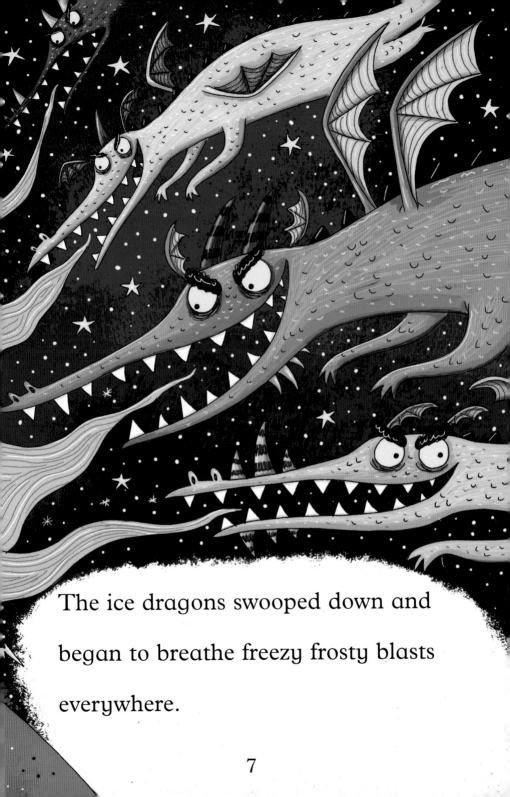

The ice dragons swooped down and began to breathe freezy frosty blasts everywhere.

'Go away!' shouted Arthur. 'Why do you come and spoil our fun?'

It was always the same.

For years and years the dragons had been coming, firing their icy blasts at the Space Knights.

The Knights had tried everything to stop them, but nothing worked. The dragons just flapped around and laughed as the Knights shivered and slipped on the ice.

'It's as slippery as my shiny shield!'

shouted Arthur. Then he got an idea.

'Hold up your shields,' he called.

So the Knights did.

As the sun shone on the shields,
its warm rays zoomed back at
the dragons.

'Hot! Hot! Hot!' puffed the dragons.

And their icy blasts began to melt.

They flapped their soggy wings

sulkily.

'Hooray, we did it!' the Knights cried. Then they danced around singing.

Ice dragons are not cool!

14

Soon, everyone began to play again.

But something was moving under

Arthur's shield.

Arthur peeped under the shield.

It was a baby ice dragon.

A Flurry of Fun

Arthur poked the baby ice dragon.

'Hey,' he whispered, 'are you OK?'

'I'm as sizzled as a sausage,' gasped

the dragon. 'I need to cool off.'

Arthur scooped ice over him. 'Aaaah, ice bath!' he said.

'I'm sorry if we hurt you,' said
Arthur. 'We just wanted to be left
alone to play.'

'I'm sorry if we spoil your games,'
said the dragon. 'We dragons don't
know any games, so we get bored.'
'I can show you some games,' said
Arthur.

Flurry was great at ten-star bowling.

He was fantastic at asteroid ball.

But best of all was ride and seek.

'Found you,' Arthur giggled.

'Today has been fun,' said Flurry.

'Hey! Maybe if I teach my family
how to play too, they won't get
bored and play tricks any more.'

'Great idea!' said Arthur.

'But, what if I forget the games?'

said Flurry.

'You won't,' said Arthur. 'Because

I'm coming with you!'

Arthur grabbed his shield, just in case.

'Now let's go on a DRAGON FUN QUEST.'

'Wheeeee!' Arthur giggled, as Flurry swooped and swerved in and out of every star and galaxy.

'Scaly planet here we come!' cried Flurry.

Slippery Slidey Delight

As they got closer they saw an army

of dragons, ready for take-off.

'Dad, it's me!' Flurry cried.

'Flurry! Where have you been?'

the Dad dragon roared.

34

He hugged Flurry, then wagged his wing at him.

'We were sending out a search party.'

He turned to Arthur.

'YOU dragon-napped my son!

So, it's nice to EAT you!'

'No, Dad! Arthur is my friend. He's

come to help us and show us how to

have fun.'

'Help *us*!' said Flurry's dad. 'Even though we play tricks on you?'

'I'd like it if we could all be friends,' said Arthur.

Then Arthur led the dragons back to the Round Planet.

'Let's teach our new friends some games,' he said to the Space Knights.

At first it was hard.

But Arthur and Flurry didn't give up.

Soon the dragons began to play

nicely and the Knights began to put

down their shields.

But then . . . oh no!

Wheeeeeeeeeeeeeeeeeeeeeeee!

'Best game . . .

'. . . **EVER!**' giggled Arthur.

'We want a turn too!' called the
other Knights.

'Dragons, do your icy trick!' shouted
Arthur.

So they did.

And soon the Round Planet was an

icy wonderland.

Now the ice dragons still come to the Round Planet and the Knights still need their shields.

But only to have fun.

Wheeeeeeeeee!